The Auction

BY

Jan Andrews

PICTURES BY

Karen Reczuch

Macmillan Publishing Company   New York

Maxwell Macmillan International Publishing Group

New York   Oxford   Singapore   Sydney

Todd jumped out of his mother's car and slammed the door.
   The things for the auction were ready on the front lawn.
The combine loomed over them.
   He pulled himself up on it and sat, high above everything.
   Just then his grandfather stepped out the front door. "Hi, Todd.
Do you want something cold to drink?" he called.

"Later," Todd muttered. He climbed down and went along the beaten track toward the barnyard. For a moment he just stood there—straining to hear the calves in the barn . . . the pigs . . . the chickens.

Then he ran through the dust, beyond the grain bins, along the trail over the summer fallow, past where the oats swayed, over the broad flat prairie to the pasture. He was looking for the cows that had been brought here every day in all the summers he could remember. There was only wind, sunshine, and dryness.

He heard his grandfather behind him.

"You sold all the animals!" Todd burst out.

"I had to."

There was something in his grandfather's voice. He saw that Gramps was crying. He began to cry, too.

Gramps put his hand on Todd's shoulder. Together they walked to the bluff.

"I loved the farm," Todd said. "And I wanted to learn it all—the combine, driving the tractor. I wanted to help you harvest. I wanted to be a farmer."

His grandfather picked up a twig and snapped it. "I can't run the place anymore. That's all there is to it." He stared ahead and smiled. "You know the first time I ever sat here?"

"When you were choosing?"

"Yeah. When I was finding a place for me and your grandma to live. It was high up and I liked it. I thought I would always be able to come here and see my land."

"And Gran?"
"She liked it, too. I brought her to see it as soon as I could manage.
We had a good time the two of us."

Todd swallowed. "Tell me all the stories."

"I've told you."

"I know, but I like them. How before you and Gran there had never been a farm here so you were pioneers, and you had to pick rocks in the spring before you put the crop in."

"How when Mom was born there was a snowstorm, and the lady
who was the helper couldn't get here. But you knew what to do—
because of the calves and stuff—and you did it and Mom was all funny
and red and wrinkled."

"We had no electricity in those days."

"But you got it. Mom was in high school, not the one-room schoolhouse anymore."

"And we kept the lights on all night so the neighbors could see, and come and help us celebrate."

Todd grinned.

"And there was the time we took wheat to the elevator. Mike
Fedak tested it. It was number two grade and you said, 'You brought
me luck, kid. I haven't seen number two in quite some while.'
You bought me an ice cream."

"Gran taught me to milk the cows."

"Once she told me to keep watch in case you came and caught her
on the swing there in the barn."

"You had fun, I bet," said Gramps. Then he leaned back and gazed
at the sky and the blueness.

They sat and told stories until the sun was almost down.

"We should go in," Gramps said.

Todd took his grandfather's hand and held it tight until they reached the house.

It was long past time for supper. There was nothing to cook and no chairs, so they sat on the floor and ate bread and cheese and pickles. The pickles were Gran's. She'd made them before she died last fall.

They had a special garden taste to them. Todd crunched one slowly and remembered his grandmother bending over the cucumbers, picking.

"There was always a scarecrow in Gran's garden," he blurted
suddenly. "And each year it was different."

"Your mother made a clown once. It set your grandmother off.
Next thing we knew we had a dancer."

"And I made a witchy lady. She didn't turn out right but Gran used her anyway.

"Gran would have made something crazy—for the auction—don't you think?" Todd said.

"We've got some old clothes in the bedroom and lots of straw out in the yard." Todd's grandfather dragged bags of clothes outside and they started to work.

When the scarecrow was finished they lifted it onto the combine.

"Let's put someone else by the sewing machine," Todd suggested.
"And a lady by the baler. And some kids."
"And maybe some sort of monsters." Todd giggled.

The moon rose higher. Stars shone in the moonlight. Todd and his grandfather worked until they had used up all the clothes and there were scarecrows everywhere.

They looked at each other. "When you're in town," Todd said, "and live near us, I'll like it." He yawned as they walked up the porch steps and into the house.

They pulled a mattress into a patch of moonlight by the window.
''Will people come early for the sale in the morning?'' Todd asked.
''They always do,'' Gramps answered.
Todd's eyes were closing. He rolled over and went to sleep.

For Mean Jean
and all her kids
—J.A.
For my own Farmers,
my grandparents
Arthur and Irene
—K.R.

Text copyright © 1990 by Jan Andrews
Illustrations copyright © 1990 by Karen Reczuch
All rights reserved. No part of this book may be reproduced
or transmitted in any form or by any means, electronic or mechanical,
including photocopying, recording, or any information storage and
retrieval system, without permission in writing from the Publisher.
Macmillan Publishing Company
866 Third Avenue, New York, NY 10022
Collier Macmillan Canada, Inc.
1200 Eglinton Avenue East, Suite 200, Don Mills, Ontario M3C 3N1
First published by Groundwood Books / Douglas & McIntyre Ltd., Toronto, Canada
First American edition 1991   Printed and bound in Hong Kong

1 2 3 4 5 6 7 8 9 10

Library of Congress CIP data is available

ISBN 0-02-705535-3